# DINOSAUR DINOSAUR

BY **Kevin Lewis** • ILLUSTRATED BY Daniel Kirk

# DINOSAUR DINOSAUR

SCHOLASTIC INC.

New York   Toronto   London   Auckland   Sydney
Mexico City   New Delhi   Hong Kong   Buenos Aires

ISBN-13: 978-0-439-91818-3
ISBN-10: 0-439-91818-9

Text copyright © 2006 by Kevin Lewis. Illustrations copyright © 2006 by Daniel Kirk.
All rights reserved. Published by Orchard Books, an imprint of Scholastic Inc.
ORCHARD BOOKS and design are registered trademarks of Watts Publishing Group, Ltd.,
used under license. SCHOLASTIC and associated logos are trademarks and/or
registered trademarks of Scholastic Inc.

12 11 10 9 8 7 6 5 4 3 2 1                           7 8 9 10 11 12/0

Printed in the U.S.A.                           40

First Scholastic paperback printing, March 2007

The art was created with gouache and colored pencil on paper.
The text type is 21-point Fink Heavy.
Type design by Richard Amari

For Alexander and Ethan. —K.L.

For Frederick, Freddy, and Casey. —D.K.

Dinosaur, dinosaur,
wake up with a roar!
Grumpy-lumpy dinosaur,
stomp across the floor!

Yummy-tummy dinosaur,
sit right down to eat.
Munchy-crunchy dinosaur,
what a breakfast treat!

Dinosaur, dinosaur,
all those teeth to brush.
Pacy-racy dinosaur,
dressing in a rush!

Ready-freddy dinosaur.
But where's your other shoe?
Looky-looky, dinosaur,
it's playing peek-a-boo!

Jumpy-bumpy dinosaur,
run outside and play.
Busy-whizzy dinosaur...

...all the livelong day!

Dinosaur, dinosaur,
laughing without care.
Funny-bunny dinosaur,
hopping everywhere!

Happy-yappy dinosaur,
running all around.

Bouncy-pouncy dinosaur,
till the sun is going down.

Dinosaur, dinosaur,
please don't run and hide!
Howdy-rowdy dinosaur,
time to go inside.

Howly-yowly dinosaur,

look, the stars are out!

Tiny-whiny dinosaur,

there's no need to pout.

Dinosaur, dinosaur,
dirty as can be.
Slurpy-burpy dinosaur,
come and dine with me.

Muddy-duddy dinosaur,
soap up in the tub.
Bubbly-wubbly dinosaur,
rub-a-dub-a-dub.

Dinosaur, dinosaur,
stumble up the stairs.
Sleepy-weepy dinosaur,
did you say your prayers?

Hazy-lazy dinosaur,
turn off all the lights.
I love you, little dinosaur,
good night, sweet dreams.

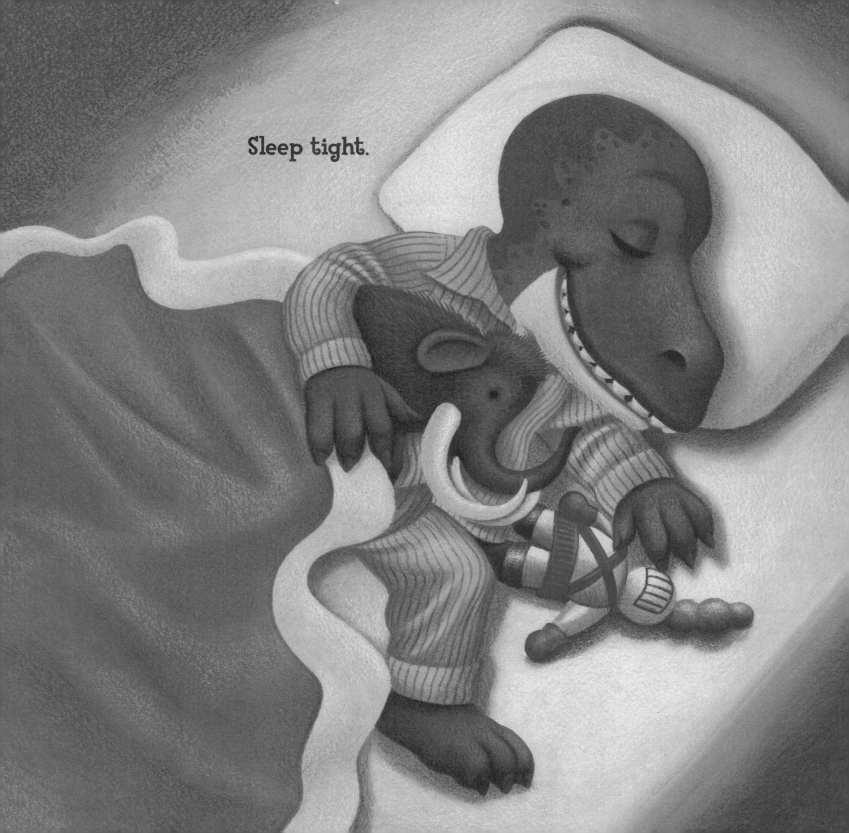

Sleep tight.